This book belongs to

To your child's messy room

Authors
Colette Stone and Elizabeth Stone

Illustrator
Daniel Naranjo

Editors
John Hansen & Millie Godwin

Colette & Eliz

2 of Us Studio

Hmm, I've had enough!
Stinker It's all too tough.
There is nothing to do,
In this messy room.

Mum has asked us to stay put.
I cannot even move my foot.

I wish she could just overlook,
The pile of dirty clothes and books.

The apple core beside my bed,
sits next to crisps and mouldy bread.

It isn't there for Stinker and me,
but for the ants who come for tea.

Mum asks, "Why are those marks on the wall?
There's no clean space. None at all!"

"Pencils, crayons, paints, and glue
to hide the stains I made with stew."

Why does mum keep going on?
It seems like she complains for fun.

What is the point of folding clothes?
And placing them in a wardrobe?
If I did not, who would know?
though some of them smell super gross

And if my clothes fall on the floor,
I just don't need them anymore.
If I should ever change my mind,
they'll be there, under toys. That's fine!

Mum says, "Harry make your bed,
so you can rest your little head."
But why is this such a big deal?
My bed gets messy again. Unreal!

My toys are placed carefully around the room,
so I can run around them - **ZOOM!**

When Stinker and I go on big adventures
we need a clear path to escape scary creatures.

Over there is where we pretend we're in space.
The one eyed aliens have their own place.

We also had fun beneath the deep blue sea,
watching sharks and dolphins swim in harmony.

And here is where Stinker jumped over the fence.
He was chased by dinosaurs; I ran to his defence.

All my toys are just where they should be,
if I have to move any it will not make me happy.

Hmm, Stinker and I are just fed up.
Cleaning rooms is just too much.

Why does mum keep going on?
It seems like she complains for fun

It is not fair that Mum blames me all the time.
Especially when Dad takes part in this crime.

He plays games with me and then disappears.
He does not say one word when Mum interferes.

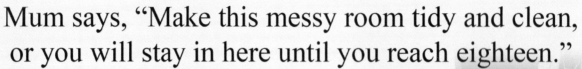

Mum says, "Make this messy room tidy and clean,
or you will stay in here until you reach eighteen."

I fold my arms, stomp my feet, and decline.
I say, "That's not how I want to spend all my time."

Hmm, Stinker and I are fed up resisting.
I have no choice. My mum keeps insisting.
I must do what mum asks and tidy my room.
Otherwise, I know Stinker and I are doomed.

I put everything back in its right place,
I cleaned up the food so there no trace.

I wash my hands well to get rid of green paint,
and remove all evidence of grime from my face.

" Mum, come quickly, I have done as I'm told. Took away my favourite frog and the fat toad".

"I even shooed away the greedy white mouse!"

Mum smiles. "Thank you Harry, you did as I asked. You've done a great job with this difficult task."

Now that my room is as clean as can be.
Mum is finally happy! Will it last? We will see.

About the Authors

Hello Everyone,
We are a mother and daughter writing duo who have used our skills, experiences, humour, combined interests, and the strong bond we share to create a collection of children's books aimed at younger readers.

After years of putting our creativity on hold and keeping our wealth of stories to ourselves, we finally took the leap of faith required of any writer and decided to bring our tales to life through the children's eyes.

With a strong emphasis on family, we write across various topics, from fictional to early childhood education, that young children are quickly able to grasp and relate to. We also incorporate life lessons in our books by using our journeys and the difficulties we faced as a multicultural family, presenting them in a fun and interactive way that we hope will inspire young readers from any background.

The essence of our books remains to capture all the memories - good and bad – we have had in life and encourage children around the world by making reading and learning fun.

Look out for more great books by the same authors, including:

• Mirror, Little Mirror, Who Are You,
• See Everyone Clearly - A Book Of Compassion Through A Child's Eye,
• My Noisy Belly - Count With Me,
• Help Me Find My Voice
• and many more!

Colette and Elizabeth Stone

Reviews are welcome and appreciated!

Printed in Great Britain
by Amazon

14961410R00025